A BOOK OF
SCARY THINGS

by Paul Showers

Illustrated by Susan Perl

Doubleday & Company, Inc.
GARDEN CITY, NEW YORK
1977

D1285618

ISBN: 0-385-12140-7 Trade
0-385-12141-5 Prebound
Library of Congress Catalog Card Number 76-11031

9   8   7   6   5   4   3   2

Lots of things are scary.
A spider is scary because it has too many legs.
A centipede is scary because it has even *more* legs.

A swimming pool is scary when you go off the high board the first time.

Even a door can scare you
if it shuts suddenly with a bang.

My sister, Peggy, is afraid of cows.

Sometimes I get scared watching TV. I'm scared even after I go to bed. I see all those things in the dark that aren't there.

I don't even dare to stick my foot out. I'm afraid there are monsters under the bed and they'll reach up and bite me. I lie as still as I can. I breathe very softly so they won't hear me and know I'm there. After a while they go away.

Sometimes I go to sleep first.

In the morning I look under the bed. Of course, there aren't any monsters there. I knew it all the time.

Just the same, I was scared.

Some people say boys should always be brave and should never be scared. But *everybody* is afraid of some things some of the time.

My grandmother is afraid of airplanes. She always has to take a pill when she takes a plane.

I know kids who are afraid of the wind. It scares them when it blows too hard and pushes them.

At night the wind can sound scary to me when it blows around the house. The wind goes "Oooooᵒᵒᵒᵒooo," and if you listen, you can hear all the bones of the house cracking. That's when I put my head under the pillow.

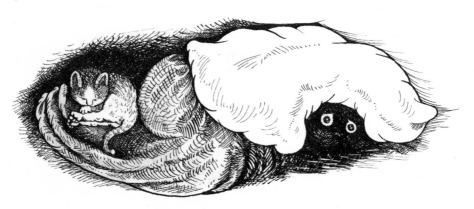

Some people are scared by loud noises. My cousin, Larry, is afraid to light the stove. He's afraid the gas will pop and blow out the match. Sometimes it does.

The man next door is afraid of cats. He chases them out of his yard. He doesn't like to have a cat anywhere near him. Even outdoors on the side-walk.

My mother is a rather brave woman. She isn't afraid of cows. She doesn't get scared when she finds a mouse in the kitchen.

But a little snake in the garden can scare her.

My father is brave, too. He isn't afraid of hornets or a fire in the oven.
But he's afraid to go up high on a ladder. He painted the downstairs part of our house. But he got his friend Bill to paint the upstairs part.

Sometimes it's a good thing to be scared. When you're not paying attention, a loud auto horn can scare you and make you jump.

That's a lot better than getting run over.

My Uncle Ned lives in Kansas. Out there, people are always scared when they see a black cloud like this hanging down out of the sky. This is a tornado.

When they see a tornado coming, the people duck down in the cellar as fast as they can. If they're driving their cars, they pull over to the side of the road and get down in the ditch.

A tornado is a terrific wind that blows everything to pieces that it touches. My uncle says anybody who isn't afraid of a tornado is crazy.

Father says it's always good to be a little scared of wild animals. On a camping trip, you should never try to feed cookies to the bears you meet.

They may look friendly, but they aren't friendly at all. They aren't afraid of you as most wild animals are. So they don't run away when you come near them. A bear would just as soon eat your hand as your cookies. So keep the cookies for yourself and don't get too close.

In a thunderstorm, the thunder isn't anything to be afraid of. It's just a loud noise in the sky. It's like the noise an airplane makes, only louder.

Thunder is the sound that lightning makes. And lightning is very dangerous. It is as bad as a tornado. You should always try to keep out of its way.

When lightning flashes down from the clouds in a storm, it often strikes things that stick up high, like trees or tall buildings. But people are safe from lightning in a tall building that is made of concrete and steel. Lightning hits the Empire State Building in New York City many times every year, but nobody inside ever gets hurt.

In a storm you are also pretty safe in a house that has lightning rods on it or in your car with the windows closed.

You should never stand under a tree in a thunderstorm, no matter how hard it is raining. It's better to lie down flat on the ground out in the open and get soaking wet than to be hit by lightning.

You shouldn't stay out on a lake in a small boat either, when there is lightning. And don't go in swimming.

Father says you ought to be careful about some things even when you aren't scared. I'm never afraid of my dog, Murphy. He likes me better than anybody else in the world. He likes to play tug of war with a stick. I pull, and he pulls back. He growls and sounds very fierce, but he is laughing with his tail.

I'm careful with Murphy when he is eating his dinner. Murphy doesn't want to play when he's eating. If you try to touch his dish, he will growl. He isn't laughing then. I let Murphy alone while he eats.

Everybody is afraid of something. Even Murphy. He is afraid of thunder. When there's a storm outside, he goes into the closet and hides.

I try to help Murphy when he's scared. I hold him and pat him. I tell him everything will be all right and not to be afraid. He shakes all over and looks very sad.

Every summer, Murphy and I go to visit one of my aunts. She lives out in the country in a big old house with lots of rooms. All day I play outdoors with Murphy and have a good time.

At night I have to go to bed upstairs. That isn't so much fun.

There's a big, spooky staircase. My bedroom is at the end of the hall. I'm afraid to go by myself because I'm afraid of the dark. I don't tell anybody because I know it's silly to be afraid. I know there aren't any monsters up there in the bedroom in my aunt's house. Still, I'm afraid to go up to bed alone.

That's when Murphy helps me. Murphy is afraid of thunder, but he isn't afraid of the dark. He seems to like it. He likes to go sniffing around.

When I go to bed, my aunt lets me take Murphy with me. He goes ahead and looks in all the corners.

He goes into the bedroom first, wagging his tail. Then I know everything is all right, and I go in and turn on the light.

After I undress and get in bed, Murphy gets in with me. He likes to sleep in the bed.

I turn out the light. I don't see any monsters in the dark anywhere. I shut my eyes and Murphy shuts his. The next thing I know—

—it's *morning!*